STINKY
AND
SUCCESSFUL

The Riot Brothers Never Stop

by MARY AMATO

illustrated by
ETHAN LONG

Holiday House / New York

Hey, Noah Albion, this one is
for you and your mom!
M. A.

I'm not sure who to dedicate this book to,
but if you happen to be stinky AND successful,
you're lucky and this book is for you.
E. L.

Text copyright © 2007 by Mary Amato
Illustrations copyright © 2007 by Ethan Long
All Rights Reserved
Printed in the United States of America
www.holidayhouse.com
3   5   7   9   10   8   6   4   2

Library of Congress Cataloging-in-Publication Data
Amato, Mary.
Stinky and successful : the Riot brothers never stop / by Mary Amato ; illustrated by
Ethan Long. — 1st ed.
p. cm.
ISBN-13: 978-0-8234-2100-8 (hardcover)
[1. Brothers—Fiction.   2. Schools—Fiction.   3. School principals—Fiction.
4. Humorous stories.]   I. Long, Ethan, ill.   II. Title.
PZ7.A49165St 2007
[Fic]—dc22
2007013366

ISBN 978-0-8234-2196-1 (paperback)

CONTENTS

Book One
THE RIOT BROTHERS RESCUE A DAMSEL IN DISTRESS

Book Two
THE RIOT BROTHERS FOOL THEIR MOM

Book Three
THE RIOT BROTHERS BECOME MAD SCIENTISTS

BONUS!

ONE

Be Nice to Your Socks!

I know what you're thinking. You just read the title of this new Riot Brother adventure and you're thinking: Rescue a damsel? Oh crud! The Riot Brothers are going to get all lovey-dovey. Well, it's not true. There's plenty of funny stuff in this story, so keep reading. Besides, if you stop reading, you'll never find out how to play a game called Knot-a-Sock and the rest of your days will be filled with sadness and despair. Knot-a-Sock is just one of the many games that I, Wilbur Riot, like to play with my socks. Just last night, I suggested to my brother, Orville, that we play it.

"Do I like that game, Wilbur?" he asked.

"Yes, of course you do," I said.

Orville is very lucky to have me for a brother because sometimes he forgets the answers to the important questions of life, such as: 1) Do I like that game? and 2) Has an elephant ever gotten a peanut stuck up his or her trunk nostril?

But Wilbur, I can hear you saying! Has an elephant ever gotten a peanut stuck up his or her trunk nostril, and how do you play Knot-a-Sock? Good questions. I'll answer, but first I have a question for you. Have you ever thought about what it would be like to be a sock? I think about being a sock. I close my eyes and imagine that I have no bones. I'm just a tube of stretchy soft stuff lying in a dark drawer. It's a good thing I'm not afraid of the dark. It would be horrible to be afraid of the dark if you were a sock. All you would be doing all day and night is thinking, please, someone open this drawer and let some light in!

Last night, I suggested the Knot-a-Sock game because Orville and I needed a break. We were having a hard time trying to decide what our mission for tomorrow would be. *(Riot Brother Rule #1: Make something exciting happen every day.)*

We sat down, facing each other. "On your mark, get set, knot!"

We lunged for each other's feet. I grabbed one of O-bro's socks and pulled on the toe part just right. You can't pull the sock off, you just have to pull until the toe part is hanging off the front of the other person's foot like a little elephant trunk. It's hard to do this just right because the other person is usually screaming and thrashing. Orville was screaming and thrashing and grabbing the toe part of my sock. But I kept my cool. Quickly I twisted the toe of his sock into a knot before he could do mine. You have to knot both of the other person's socks in order to win.

"YI-I-I-I-I-I!" He screamed, then started laughing. Trust me. There is something about having your sock tied in a knot while it's still on your foot that feels very funny. Orville was doomed. I mean, once you start to laugh it's hard to get control. So, I grabbed his other foot and tied that sock into a knot, which made him laugh so hard that he started snorting. He stuck his feet in the air, and we both howled. His feet looked like they were wearing odd little crowns.

"I won!" I laughed triumphantly and stuck

my feet in the air. Orville jumped up and wrestled my right sock into a knot.

Our mom walked in. "What now?" she groaned.

Orville smiled sweetly. "If you were a sock, wouldn't you want someone to play a game with you now and then?"

Mom laughed. "Well, it's time for you and your socks to go to bed."

"But we haven't chosen our secret mission for tomorrow," he argued.

"Well, that will have to wait. It's not my fault you decided to knot each other up."

"Yes, Orville," I said. "Stop being so knotty."

"Very pun-ny," Mom said.

"I don't get it, Wilbur," Orville said.

"Knotty. Naughty," I said.

"Do you guys get it?" Orville asked his socks. They didn't answer. Which reminds me. You asked a question that I haven't answered yet. Has a peanut ever gotten stuck up the trunk nostril of an elephant? I have no idea. Tell me when you find out! Now, go to bed!

May We Helpeth You?

Did you go to bed? I had to. And I must have fallen asleep because I was sleeping peacefully when a voice shattered the morning silence.

"Wake up, you slumbering clod!"

I opened my eyes.

Orville was standing on my bed, bellowing at me. "Wake up, I say! Time is wasting!"

Usually I like it when Orville wakes me

up. But getting yelled at was a little much. I rubbed my eyes. "Did you just call me a clod?"

Orville took a deep breath and struck a pose. "I, Orville the Riot, have chosen our mission for the day." He pretended to blow a trumpet. "Hear ye! Hear ye! On this day, the Brothers Riot shall rescue a damsel in distress!" He waited for my reaction.

"You've got to be kidding."

"Kidding I am not."

"That's a lame mission, Orville."

"'Tis not! 'Tis noble, Wilbur."

"I think you've been reading too many of those King Arthur stories, Orville. Why would you want to rescue a damsel in distress?"

"Because that's how you become a knight, and I've always wanted to be a knight."

He obviously didn't understand the whole situation. "Do you realize that what a knight usually gets is a damsel's hand in marriage?" I asked.

Orville looked suitably horrified. "Why would I want another hand? I've got two of my own right here."

My point exactly.

"Let's pick another topic," I suggested.

"We can't. I already wrote it down."

"What?"

He showed me the *Secret Riot Brother Mission Book* where we write down our missions. We had a new rule.

Riot Brother Rule #16:
You have to write down
your mission of the day.

We made it up because we were getting into arguments and changing our minds and Riot Brother Rule #5 is Don't change your mission in the middle of the day.

"Guess it's too late," Orville said.

I sighed deeply. "We must go forward with this mission. We cannot change that rule. But we'll make up a new rule. Riot Brother Rule Number Seventeen: If you rescue a damsel in distress, you do not have to marry her."

Orville looked suitably relieved.

I went on. "Now, as you know, Rule Number Two states that we cannot tell anyone our true mission, so we cannot tell a damsel that we are rescuing her from distress. We just have to do it."

"But how will we know if she is in distress?"

"I guess we can ask her if she's distressed. But then we have to zip our lips and just undistress her."

"Bingo bongo, Wilbur!"

We went down to breakfast.

Mom was just finishing her tea and toast.

"What about her?" Orville whispered. "Since we don't have to marry her, she could count as a damsel, couldn't she?"

"There's only one problem," I whispered back.

"She's too old?"

"No. She doesn't look distressed."

"Uh-oh. I hear whispering," Mom said. "That usually means trouble."

"How are you this morning, Mom?" Orville asked. "Are you distressed?"

"I'm just dandy," Mom said, turning a page of her newspaper.

"Rats," Orville said.

"Sorry to disappoint you, kiddo."

"Should we whisper some more, Wilbur?" Orville whispered. "That seemed to distress her a little."

"I don't think we're supposed to distress the You-Know-Who first. I think we're supposed to find her already distressed," I whispered back.

"Right," Orville nodded. "Call if any distress pops up, okay, Mom?"

Mom laughed. "Deal."

We went to school early, of course, and sat outside on the bench, looking for damsels in possible distress.

14

Margaret Lew arrived, carrying her trombone case.

Seeing a real live girl made me wonder about this whole damsel-in-distress idea. First of all, the girls I know can rescue themselves. Second of all, what if girls thought we wanted to help them because we were in love with them? That would be terrible. Then we would be distressed. And who would rescue us?

A little voice inside me said, "Retreat! Retreat!" But then a louder voice that was even deeper inside me said, "You are a Riot Brother, and it is your duty to follow the Riot Brother Rules." Then another voice added, "Just go with the flow, dude." It's kind of crowded in my head.

While I was listening to my inner voices, Orville's inner knight came charging out.

"Lady Margaret, that looks distressingly heavy!" Orville jumped up and grabbed the trombone case out of her hand . . . and then he dropped it on her foot.

"YOW!" she screamed. For a damsel, Margaret can really let one loose.

"Sorry," Orville said.

"Oh, by the way, Margaret," I called out as she began limping in. "We're all going on that field trip, remember? So you didn't have to bring your trombone."

"Urggh," she said, which I guess is what you say when you're angry at yourself for lugging in a trombone case for nothing.

Ms. Geary, the art teacher, arrived next with her arms full of supplies.

"Wow," I said. "Here comes a definite damsel in distress!"

She must have heard it because she laughed. "I can't say I've ever been called that before. Will you boys help me with the door?"

"We shall and we will, fair lady!" Orville cried.

What happened next was really a good thing if you think about it in a certain way. See, if we had succeeded in helping Ms. Geary, then our mission would have been over and there wouldn't be any story; and if there weren't any story, you wouldn't have funny stuff to read; and if you didn't have funny stuff to read, you would flunk out of school and your parents would be distressed; and if your parents were distressed, they would lose their jobs and cry; and if everyone cried, the dirt would turn to mud, which would make all the worms come out; and then the birds would eat so many worms, they'd be too fat to fly; and then the cats would eat so many birds, they'd be too fat to chase after the mice; and so the mice would take over the world, which would be great if you were a mouse, but not so great if you were, say, a piece of cheese.

So, really, it was a good thing for cheese that Orville and I both jumped to get the door. But

I'm not so sure Ms. Geary would say that it was a good thing that I accidentally tripped her just as Orville was swinging open the door because the door kind of smashed into her and she got splattered with a little purple paint.

Okay, it wasn't a *little* paint. Her glasses were purple. Her dress was purple. Even her shoes were purple. It was a *lot* of paint.

"Isn't purple your favorite color?" Orville asked hopefully.

"It used to be," she said, pushing a strand of purple hair off her purple face.

After we apologized and helped her clean up, Orville asked if the clean up would count as a rescue from distress.

"No, Orville," she said.

We could not try to rescue any more damsels because the bell rang.

"Orville," I said as I wiped the last of the paint off the door. "I have to admit, I'm kind of glad to hear that old bell ring. This rescuing business is a lot of work."

Orville sighed. "I knoweth what you mean, O goodly Wilbur."

He looked so sad, I thought I would try to cheer him up. "Well, if they made kids into knights just for talking like one, thou would most certainly win, O goodly brother. For a third grader, thou art not too shabby."

"Your words are liketh chocolate to my ears!" Orville said.

"I think you mean that my words are to your ears like chocolate is to your tummy."

"Do you have any chocolate?" Orville asked.

Sadly, I had to shake my head.

"If I did, I certainly wouldn't put it in my ears," Orville added. "Why are we talking about chocolate anyway?"

"You brought it up!"

"I did?" He sighed. "Well, I have goodly taste." He bowed. "Farewell, O Wilbur, until we meet again!"

THREE

Hark! What Is That Brilliant Song I Hear?

Have you ever wondered why field trips are called field trips? Have you ever wondered who invented them? Was the first field trip to a field and is that why they are called field trips? Or perhaps a smart and fun-loving teacher named Mr. or Ms. Field invented the field trip and named it after him- or herself? Some people might think you have a big head if you call it a field trip because that's your name, but I think it's completely understandable. Orville and I have named many things after ourselves, and we don't have big heads. Actually we do have big heads, but it's not because we're conceited. It's because our brains are HUMONGOUS! You'd think that with heads as big as ours, we'd have sore necks, but it's the poor kids who sit behind us in class who have the sore necks. They have to keep looking around us to see the teacher!

The good news is that everybody loves our big heads because our brains are always full of great ideas. Don't take my word for it. For example, what were Margaret, Jonathan, Selena, and Alan doing on the field-trip bus on the way to the Botanic Garden? They

were all singing one of the famous Riot Brother Songs.

Someday soon Orville and I plan to publish *The Riot Brother Songbook*. Once it hits the streets, everyone will want to sing the songs and the world will become a happy place with people laughing instead of crying and then cheese will be really safe. Orville and I may even win an award for saving the world with our music.

I'm getting so excited just thinking about it that I can't wait for the book to come out. I'm going to give you a sneak preview. For maximum enjoyment, act out this song while singing it.

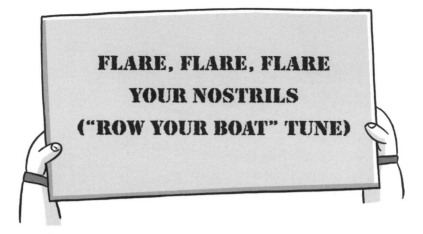

FLARE, FLARE, FLARE YOUR NOSTRILS ("ROW YOUR BOAT" TUNE)

(Special Warning: Our mom read this and said that we should remind you that bus drivers work very hard for your safety and that you must NOT give them a hard time. If you are riding a bus, you must remain seated AT ALL TIMES. So that means you must wiggle your rear while remaining seated, which is totally possible. If you don't believe me, try wiggling your rear right now. Ha ha! Made you do it!)

Okay, I know what you're thinking. You're thinking, *That nostril song is a masterpiece!* Since you liked it, I'll teach you one more. (Special Warning: Do NOT act this one out by taking off your pants! Ha ha.)

OUR PANTS GO MARCHING ("THE ANTS GO MARCHING" TUNE)

This is a great one to sing in a crowd, even if nobody takes off any pants, because it's always funny to sing about underwear.

Orville and I have made up lots of funny songs over the years. And on the way to the Botanic Garden, we sang them all to the delight of our bus driver, I'm sure. After we came to a complete stop in the parking lot, I stood up and said, "Wait! I feel a saying coming on."

Everyone listened politely. Well, except for the bus driver, who for some reason ran off the bus.

"Singing a song is like taking your voice on a field trip," I said. "It deserves to have a little fun."

There were nods of agreement all around.

After I got off the bus, Orville pulled me aside and whispered, "'Tis true what you said about goodly singing, O Wilbur! But fie! We haveth a problem on our hands."

"What's the problem?" I asked.

"We sang so many goodly songs, we forgot all about rescuing a damsel."

I nodded wisely. "Let us make haste and

keep our eyes open. Perhaps we shall find a damsel in yonder garden!"

I could tell that he liked the way I said "make haste" and "yonder" because of his face. His face was giving me the Hey-It's-Not-Too-Shabby-Having-You-For-a-Brother look. I have to admit that it's a very nice look to get from a brother.

FOUR

Why Would You Want Hair on Your Toes?

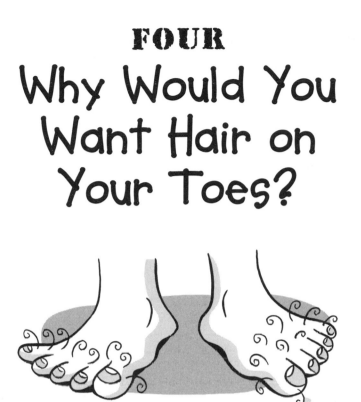

In case you were wondering, it's not easy to get a tan at the Botanic Garden. I thought it would be. I thought that was the whole point. As it turns out, the Botanic Garden isn't even outside. It's INSIDE! It's like a big indoor zoo but instead of looking at animals, you're looking at plants. There aren't any cages, so you could walk right up and touch some of these plants, but I suggest you don't because some of them have spikes and some of them have poisonous leaves and some of them would sadly rip if everybody touched them. So keep your dirty rotten hands off the plants, will you?

The main room of the Botanic Garden has a shallow little stream running through it. No kidding. It's like the outside is inside. There are dragonflies and ladybugs and even birds flying around, and the air is misty. When we arrived, a little girl was standing on a low wooden footbridge with her mommy, peering into the stream. All was quiet. And then the little girl started jumping up and down and yelling, "Foggy! Foggy!"

"Hark!" Orville cried. "Methinks I hear a girl distressed because of the fog!"

Orville dashed for the bridge before I could stop him. He was concentrating so hard on the girl that he didn't see the wet leaf on the bridge. His foot hit it and he slid.

In baseball, that's called sliding into home base. In the Botanic Garden, that's called sliding into a little girl's face. He knocked the girl right off the bridge, and she fell into the water with a splash!

"WHAT ARE YOU DOING, Orville?" Mrs. Pensky cried. Mrs. Pensky is Orville's teacher.

"I was trying to help the little girl. She was distressed because of the fog," he explained.

"Fog? What fog?" the girl's mom asked as she lifted the soggy, surprised kid out of the water. "She was saying 'foggy' because she was excited to see a *froggy*."

I could tell that Orville felt bad enough, so I didn't mention the little fact that I think the girl may have squished the froggy. But Mrs. Pensky didn't think Orville felt bad enough, so she made him sit in the corner near the *Stapelia gigantea.* It's bad enough to have to sit still when you're on a field trip. But to sit near a *Stapelia gigantea* is really bad. Why, you ask? Because the *Stapelia gigantea* is a plant that has a huge flower that stinks worse than a dead skunk's socks! (Sorry, that wasn't a very nice thing to say

about socks. I bet they can't help stinking if they're on a dead skunk.)

"I hope Mrs. Pensky doesn't tell the school principal that I am having this little time-out," Orville said. I hoped so, too, for Orville's sake. In case you didn't know it, the school principal is our mom, Lydia Riot.

I had to roam the rooms of the garden and keep my eye out for possibly distressed damsels without Orville. Here's what I saw.

WHAT I SAW ON MY FIELD TRIP:
1. *Whitey-tighties sticking out of the back of Jonathan's pants!*
2. *A small black bug or perhaps a poppy seed sticking in between Margaret's two front teeth!*
3. *Hair on the toes of Mrs. Pensky! (She was wearing sandals.)*
4. *No damsels in distress!*

I could only hope that Orville had better luck.

When our classes met in the big room, I searched his face for signs of success. Alas! Alack! His face looked awful.

In the meantime, he was searching my face for signs of success.

"We're doomed, aren't we?" he said sadly.

Just then my classmate Goliath Hyke walked by. Goliath is a bully who I wish would move to another town. As Goliath walked by, he said, "You're not only doomed, Orville. You're dumb. You're dumb as a crumb." He said it very loudly so that as many people as possible would hear. He likes making people feel as low as a fly on a stinking *Stapelia gigantea.*

Everyone looked at Orville.

Riot Brother Rule #18:
If someone puts your brother down,
stick up for him.

"Goliath," I said. "If you want to call Orville a crumb, first you have to deal with me."

He stuck out his chest. "I can deal with you, punk."

"Got any cards?" I asked.

"Hunh?"

I shrugged. "How can you deal with me if you don't have any cards?"

Everybody laughed . . . well, except Goliath.

"Nice one," Jonathan Kemp whispered.

"You're dumb as a crumb, too," Goliath muttered, and wandered off.

"We don't mind being dumb and crumby," I called after him. "Because at least we're yummy."

"I feel a saying coming on," Orville said. I almost fainted. Orville has never felt a saying coming on before. We all listened politely as he cleared his throat. "If someone tries to bug you," he said wisely, "don't let it bug you."

"Not too shabby, little bro." I clapped him on the back.

Just then Goliath shouted out, "Gotcha!"

"He's got a dragonfly!" Selena cried. "Goliath, let it go. How would you like it if some big old giant caught you?"

"Mind your own business," Goliath said. "I just want to pull off its wings."

Imagine being trapped inside the sweaty paws of Goliath Hyke. What worse prison could there be?

I looked at Orville. Orville looked at me. I could see it in his eyes. He was thinking the same thing I was thinking: It was time for Operation Armpit. This is a secret Riot Brother strategy that we save for serious situations. Doing it successfully requires the courage to stick your hands where no hands want to go. We lunged for Goliath, stuck our hands in his armpits, and tickled.

"Stop it!" he screamed. His arms flew

apart, and the dragonfly zipped out of his hands.

Everyone cheered. Well, except Goliath. He stuck his hands under his armpits and stomped away.

"Looks like Operation Armpit worked," I said.

Orville sighed. "We rescued the dragonfly. Why can't we rewrite our mission to say that our goal was to rescue bugs from distress?"

"That would be cheating."

"I bet bugs would like us."

A fly landed on Orville's nose. "They already do, bro."

FIVE

Muddy Shoulders Are a Small Price to Pay

"Goliath!" Mrs. Pensky called. "You can sit next to me on the bus. Come along, children."

As we began walking toward the exit, a gardener stopped us. She had on an official muddy shirt and muddy pants and muddy gloves and even muddier boots, and on top of all that she had leaves in her hair and a smear of dirt that went from her nose all the way to her ear. In other words, she was my kind of woman. "Good job, boys. I saw the whole thing," she said. "That's one lucky damsel."

I couldn't believe my ears. "What did you just say?"

With her trowel, she gestured toward Goliath's most recent victim, which was now darting near the stream. "That's a damselfly. It looks like a dragonfly, but it's skinnier and it holds its wings up instead of out."

I looked at Orville. Orville looked at me. Our jaws were hanging so low a couple of damsels could have flown right in.

"Dost thou mean to tell me that we just rescued a damsel in distress?" I asked.

She laughed. "I guess you did."

"That means we can becometh knights!" Orville cried.

The gardener laughed again. "I hereby make you knights of the Botanic Garden." She tapped us on our shoulders with the end of her trowel.

"We did it!" I cried.

"Bingo bongo!" Orville cried.

"Get moving, boys!" Mrs. Pensky cried.

"Thank you, Official Gardener," I said.

"Yes," Orville joined in. "Thank you and farewell!"

SIX
Stop Sniffling!

After our exciting day, we came home and ate dinner. (Mom said we had to eat with forks even though we tried to explain to her that back in knightly days people ate with their fingers.) Then we messed around until bedtime.

After Mom tucked us in and left, Orville stuck his socky feet in the air and said, "I'm not tired and neither are my goodly socks."

"Let's play Sock Me a Story," I suggested.

"I'll go first," Orville whispered, whipping off his socks and rolling them into a ball. By the way, he wasn't whispering because sock stories are supposed to be secret; he was whispering because we were supposed to be sleeping and didn't want to get caught.

"*Once upon a time there was a pair of goodly white socks,*" Orville began. "*They wanted to see the world. So they hopped out of their drawer and ran into yonder street. Vroom! A huge truck ranneth over them. After the truck was gone, they peeled themselves off the road. They were not white socks any longer. They had black stripes.*" Orville threw the sock ball at me. That meant I had to add to his story.

I jumped right in. "*Then along came a*

zebra. 'Look! A pair of striped socks to match my handsome legs!' the zebra said. He put on the socks and galloped all the way to Africa. And so the socks did see the world after all. And then they were eaten by a lion. The end."

"Not too shabby!" Orville said. "Now it's your turn to start. Knock my socks off."

I flared my nostrils a few times. Sometimes that helps me get in the mood for telling a good story.

"Many moons ago, there was a poor green sock who was always wet from crying because he had lost his goodly brother."

Orville grabbed the sock ball. *"The end!"* Orville sniffled. "'Twas a sad, sad tale."

"I'm not done, dude!" I threw my pillow at him and grabbed the sock ball back. *"One day the green sock decided to try to find his brother. He walked all over town, which was very painful without shoes! After a while he went to the zoo. There was an elephant who was sniffling."* I paused and threw the sock ball at Orville.

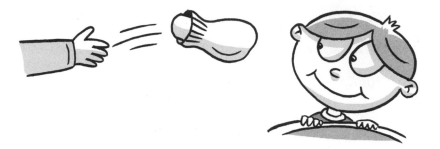

"'Why art thou sniffling?' the sock asked.

"'Because I have a peanut stuck up my trunk nostril,' the elephant said. 'Every time I sniffle, it goes a little farther in! Which makes me sniffle even more. I can't stop!'

"The sock jumped through the bars, wrapped himself around the end of the peanut, and yanked it out.

"'Hurray!' The happy elephant lifted the sock up high with his trunk. Just then, a voice called out, 'Brother! I see you!' High in the air, the green sock could see his brother running toward him. His brother had been looking for him, too!" Orville stopped and whipped the sock ball back at me.

I continued. "'Hurray!' The elephant set down the sock, and his brother ran through the

bars to him. It was such a happy sight that the elephant began to sniffle with joy. Unfortunately, his trunk was very close to the socks and he sniffled them up his nostrils." I threw the sock ball back to Orville.

He grinned. *"And so if you visit the zoo, you will see an elephant with two green socks hanging out of his trunk nostrils. And that is the end."*

Orville started cracking up but had to stop because we heard our mom's footsteps.

She opened the door. "Good night, boys."

"You mean, good night, knights," Orville said.

"Oh brother," she said.

"You mean, oh brothers," I said.

"Just go to sleep!" She closed the door.

I sighed. I had that happy feeling you get when you've just had a good day, and it's not quite over because you're still awake.

Orville shined his secret Riot Brother flashlight at me and whispered, "Hey Wilbur, are you asleep?"

Riot Brother Rule #19:
Always keep a flashlight
under your pillow.

"Not yet," I whispered back.

"I know that rescuing a damsel wasn't your favorite mission, but you stood by me. So I just want you to know that if you ever get stuck in an elephant's nostril, I will come and pull you out."

I shone my flashlight at him. "Thank you, Orville."

"Unless I'm stuck in there, too," he added. "If we're both stuck, we'll just have to wait until we're so slimy with elephant snot that we slide right out."

"Well, if that happens, at least we can keep each other goodly company," I said.

We gave each other looks of brotherly love. Then we threw our stinking socks at each other.

The End

ONE

I Forget What This Chapter Is Called

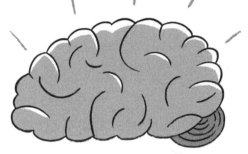

Hip hip hooray for homework!

Are you wondering if I have lost my mind? Perhaps cruel teachers from outer space have invaded my head and removed my brain?

First of all, thank you for being worried about me. But you can relax. I still have my good old amazing brain, and it's working fine. Let me explain why I'm hip-hip-hooraying for homework.

It all started with a problem late last

night. I was lying in bed, looking up at the ceiling, trying to remember what it was that I was trying to remember. Have you ever had that problem?

"Orville?" I whispered. "Are you asleep?"

"Yes," he whispered back.

"You know how it is when you know that there's something important, only you don't know what it is?"

"No."

"Well, I'm trying to remember what it is that I forgot."

He flicked on his flashlight and beamed it on my face. "Did you forget that you have a loose tooth?"

"Oh yeah, I did!" I wiggled my tooth. "But that isn't it."

"Did you forget that you forgot to take out the garbage?"

"Oops! I did. But that isn't it, either."

"Did you forget that you owe me ten dollars?"

"You owe *me* ten dollars, Orville."

"Oh yeah. I forgot that I was hoping you'd forget." He quickly changed the subject. "Did you forget that you forgot to do your homework?"

"Rats on rye!" I yelped. "I did forget to do my homework! That still isn't it, but I better do it."

I got my flashlight and a pencil and wrote my name and the date on a piece of paper.

That's when I finally remembered what I had forgotten! I almost jumped right out of my pajamas. "Orville, our favorite holiday is tomorrow!"

"Halloween?"

"Orville, today is March thirty-first. How could it be Halloween?"

"You're the one who said it was Halloween."

"No I didn't. I said our favorite holiday is tomorrow."

"Exactly! Our favorite holiday is Halloween."

"Wrong! Our favorite holiday is April Fools' Day, which is tomorrow."

"It is?"

"Yes. We've got to stay up very late tonight planning. Our mission is clear."

"It is?"

"Yes. What do we try and fail to do every April Fools' Day?"

"I forget."

"Fool Mom."

"Yeah. Somehow she always gets us!"

"Precisely! This year, our mission will be to fool her!"

We got out our *Secret Riot Brother Mission Book* and wrote down our mission. Then we made a list of all the things we would try to do to fool our dear old mom. I'm not going to show you the list yet because if I did then you would know exactly what is going to happen in this book, and it wouldn't be as much fun to read.

When we were done with our list, Orville's eyes practically popped out of their sockets. "I just remembered something really important that we both forgot!" he exclaimed.

"What is it?" I asked.

This was serious. I could tell by Orville's face.

"We forgot to eat dessert," he said.

A chill went up my spine. This *was* serious.

Riot Brother Rule #20:
Never ever go to bed
without eating dessert.

"We can't break a Riot Brother rule!" I ex-claimed. "Let's go!" We tiptoed downstairs to the kitchen. Thank goodness our mom was practicing her cello in the den.

"Guess what I'm in the mood for?" Orville asked.

"Fish guts on toast?"

"No. I'm in the mood for a Loud Cloud."

I know what you're thinking. You're thinking, what is a Loud Cloud? It's a Riot Brother Edible Invention.

"We can't have Loud Clouds because we have to be quiet," I whispered.

"Then let's have Quiet Clouds," Orville said. "They're not as much fun, but they're tasty."

Orville got a can of whipped cream out of the refrigerator and read the instructions. "Shake before using." He held the can in one hand and shook his body all over. Then he stuck out his tongue and squirted a big cloud of whipped cream onto his tongue. To make a

Loud Cloud, you have to sing as loudly as you can while squirting, which is the really fun part; but Orville kept it to a soft *aaaah* and handed me the can.

We were both aaaahing with big gobs of delicious fluffy clouds of cream on our tongues when something horrible happened. The cello music stopped. We heard foot-steps.

"Whhuuuh!" Orville said, which is what *"Run!"* sounds like when your mouth has a cloud in it.

TWO

A Sprinkle of Sugar?

Did you know that scientists have recently discovered that poisonous jumping spiders like to burrow deep in between the pages of books because they like the taste of the glue that holds the books together? Don't look too closely in this book because if you actually see one, it will leap off the page and jump into your nostril. . . .

Did you look? April fool! Ha ha!

I just love April Fools' Day. Today I woke up earlier than Orville, which was good because I had a secret plan. I found my best plastic spider and tied a long string on it. Then quietly I tied it to the lamp next to his bed and arched the lamp so that the spider was hanging down very close to the back of Orville's head. Then I poked him.

"Orville, get out of bed quick!" I said. "There's a huge spider about to bite the back of your head."

Orville gave me his famous I-Don't-Believe-You look. "Ha ha," he said. "I'm not going to fall for that trick. It's April Fools' Day. There's no spider. You're just trying to get me to jump out of bed. See—" He turned and saw that big old spider when he was expecting to see nothing, and, boy, did he scream and jump out of bed.

I rolled on the floor laughing. Ah, what a sweet way to begin the day.

He threw his pillow at me. "Good one, Wilbur. But you know I'm going to get you when you least expect it."

"Don't count on it, O-bro. Let's not forget, I'm older and wiser than you."

We got dressed, and I led the way downstairs.

"Wilbur, you have a huge hole in the back of your pants."

I turned and shook my older and wiser head. "Orville. Orville. Orville. You think I'm going to fall for that one?"

He smiled and shrugged. "It's a free world. Flash your whitey-tighties if you want."

We crept down to the kitchen.

"What's that delicious smell?" Orville asked. "Is Mom baking something?"

"Whatever it is, it's a trick. Come on."

Mom was in the shower, which was great! Not only did it mean that she wouldn't be stinky all day, but it also meant that we had time to implement Plan #1. We put salt in the sugar bowl and sugar in the salt shaker. Our poor mother would stir "sugar" into her tea and take a big sip! Ha ha! After we were done with the switcheroo, we tiptoed back upstairs and waited until we heard her banging around in the kitchen. Then we walked down again, looking just like a pair of sleepy angels.

"Good morning, boys!" she said. She poured herself a cup of tea.

"Good morning." We yawned. The suspense was almost killing us. She set the teapot down . . . and reached for the sugar bowl . . . and at the last second picked up the salt shaker and sprinkled sugar into her tea.

"RATS!" Orville cried. "How did you know?"

Mom smiled ever so sweetly. "I used to try that one on my mother every year. Must be in the genes."

"Next year, let's put the sugar in her jeans," Orville said.

"We must move on to Plan Number Two," I whispered.

Orville nodded. "You stay here. I'll go get ready."

"You guys might as well stop trying. You're never going to get me," Mom called out as Orville ran upstairs. Then she turned to me. "Now, Wilbur, I'm making one of your favorites for breakfast today . . . a Dutch Baby! It'll be ready in about seven minutes."

In case you were wondering, a Dutch Baby is not a real baby. A Dutch Baby is a delicious kind of puffy popover treat. But that's beside the point. The point is that there was no Dutch Baby. "Ha!" I guffawed. "You think I'm going to fall for that old trick? You never make Dutch Babies on a school day. I will get breakfast for myself, thank you."

I was forcing myself to swallow burned toast when a scream shattered the silence. This was accompanied by a loud thud out the window.

These two sounds would make any normal parent call an ambulance. Our mom just sat there and opened the newspaper.

"What was that?" I asked.

"I didn't hear anything," Mom said.

The sound of moaning came next.

"Is that Orville outside?"

Mom shrugged.

I ran out. Orville was lying in the middle of the driveway, wailing and holding on to his leg, which was dripping with blood. "I fell out the window," he gasped.

"MOM!" I screamed. "Orville is really hurt!"

I knelt down next to my brother. "Hold on, little bro. Help is on the way." Tears fluttered out of my weepy eyes.

Orville grabbed my shirt. "Wilbur, I'm okay. It's just ketchup, remember?"

"I know!" I whispered. "I'm acting!"

Mom stuck her head out the window. I sobbed. "Help, he's bleeding to death!"

She laughed. "Good try. Orville, wash all that ketchup off."

"RATS AGAIN!" Orville picked himself up off the ground. "This may be our toughest mission yet."

I picked up the garbage can lid that Orville had thumped against the driveway to make the sound of himself falling out the window and put it back on the garbage can. "We must move on to Plan Number Three. Too bad we have school today."

When we got back inside, Orville went to wash up. The phone rang. I stayed in the kitchen and listened because, right away, I could tell the call was serious. "Yes, this is Lydia Riot. . . . Water pipes? . . . Just one? . . . All? . . . What does this mean? . . . Flooded? . . . How long? . . . Today? Are you sure? . . . Yes, I understand. . . . I will make the calls. . . . Thank you. Bye."

Mom turned to me with a dazed look on her face.

"What happened, Mom?" I asked.

"The water pipes at the school burst. We have to cancel school for today."

My smile practically broke my face in half. I raced into the bathroom and punched the shower curtain. "Orville, school is canceled!"

He stuck his wet head out. "What?"

"Water pipes burst! The school is flooded!"

I threw Orville a towel, and we danced out of the bathroom . . . and there was Mom staring at us with a big grin on her face. "April fool!" Then she added, "Wilbur, you need to take out the garbage, and that's no joke."

Did I mention that she was wearing oven mitts and holding the most perfectly luscious big old Dutch Baby?

THREE
Let the Cool Air In!

Plan #3 was going to take place at lunchtime and involved Slobber.

What do you mean by that, you ask? That's for me to know and you to find out!

First, we had to get through a morning of classes.

Orville headed to Mrs. Pensky's room,

and I headed to Mr. Peabody's room, which both happened to be in the same direction. As we walked down the hallway, our friend Alan caught up with us. "Wilbur, did you know that you have a hole in your pants?" he whispered.

I looked at Orville.

"I tried to tell you, bro," he said.

That Orville. He was good. He had obviously told Alan to keep the joke going. I looked Alan in the eye. "Orville put you up to this, didn't he?"

Just then I heard the horrible sound of Goliath Hyke's laughter coming from behind me. "I see London. I see France. I see Wilbur's underpants," he bellowed.

That's when doubt started to gnaw a hole in my confidence. Very casually, I rubbed my hand over the back of my blue jeans. I did have a hole! It was the size of London and France put together.

I know what you're thinking. You're wondering what YOU should do if you ever go to school and discover that you have a hole in your pants. I was wondering the same thing. "Riot Brother Rule Number Twenty-one!" I whispered to Orville.

Riot Brother Rule #21:
If your brother is ever in an embarrassing
situation, help him out of it.

Orville began wiggling his bottom and singing. "Our fine bottoms got air conditioning, air conditioning, air conditioning. Our fine bottoms got air conditioning. That's why we like to put holes in our pants!" He looked like a complete lunatic.

"This is your idea of helping?" I asked.

"Riot Brother Rule Number Twenty-two!" he whispered.

Riot Brother Rule #22:
If your brother ever makes an embarrassing
situation even more embarrassing
while trying to help you out of it,
you MUST help him in return.

There was only one thing for me to do: join in. We sang at the top of our lungs and wiggled at the bottom of our bottoms: "Our

fine bottoms got air conditioning, air conditioning, air conditioning. Our fine bottoms got air conditioning. That's why we like to put holes in our pants!"

When we stopped, our fellow students clapped. They loved it! Except for Goliath Hyke, who just grumbled and stomped off to class.

"Wait," I said. I felt a saying coming on.

Orville listened politely.

"The great advantage to being weird most of the time is that when you are weird, no one thinks it's weird."

"Bingo bongo, Wilbur."

We hurried to our classes.

My teacher, Mr. Peabody, had a big stack of papers on his desk. "Please take your seats!" he said. "We have a lot to get through today."

Just then the voice of the principal came over the intercom. "Good morning, students.

If you recall, today we will be taking the AIDYL TOIR Intelligence Tests all day."

We all groaned.

"Teachers will begin passing out papers, test-side down. Do not turn the papers over until I say you can begin."

Mr. Peabody began passing out the papers.

I stared at the blank side. Through it I could see all the faint marks of the evil test questions on the other side. I would hate to be a test. Nobody likes you. And you're only used once.

"This is just one sheet," Mr. Peabody said. "We have seventeen to do before we get a break."

Everybody moaned again. This was going to be a horrible day.

The principal said, "Turn the papers over and begin."

THE AIDYL TOIR INTELLIGENCE TEST

1. What color do you get when you mix red with red?

2. What is the name of the United States of America?

3. What year was sand invented?

4. What do monkeys say to each other when they are falling out of trees?

5. Who was tricked by the principal into taking a fake test on April 1st?

Lydia Riot got us again!

FOUR
Slobber and Frank

There is an old Riot Brother saying. Perhaps you have heard it: *The world would be a better place if all children had a roof over their head, food in their stomach, a smile in their heart, and a fake rat in their pocket.*

When it was time for lunch, Orville and I asked to go to the bathroom. We didn't really have to go. It was all part of the plan. We met in the bathroom. "Do you have Slobber?" I asked.

"That's disgusting! Do I? Where?" Orville looked at his face in the mirror.

"Not slobber!" I groaned. "Slobber!"

"Oh . . . Slobber!" He pulled our fake pet rat named Slobber out of his pocket and then stuffed her back in.

We happen to know that the school principal always eats lunch with the teachers in the lounge. We also happen to know that the secretary always stays at the front desk in order to answer the phones and keep sneaky children from sneaking into the principal's office. So, we had to be extra sneaky. I walked in first. "Mrs. Monday!" I said. Yes, that is her real name. "Mrs. Monday, there is a really cute puppy out by the flagpole." We also happen to know that Mrs. Monday loves puppies.

Too bad Mrs. Monday isn't our mom. She's so easy to fool. She went running out; and Orville snuck in. I went out to keep Mrs. Monday distracted, but the most amazing thing was that there *was* a puppy outside! The Kemps got a puppy, and Jonathan's mom was out walking her. Mrs. Monday stayed out there to talk, so I went in.

Orville was just putting Slobber in the pencil drawer of our mom's desk. "See you later, Slobby," he said, and closed the drawer.

I gave him the thumbs-up. We both turned to leave and bumped right into . . . Mom.

"Well, what can I do for you boys?" she asked.

I looked at Orville. Orville looked at me. "We just came to congratulate you on that great trick with the tests," I said. "Wasn't that a fabulous trick, Orville?"

"It certainly was, Wilbur. Just fabulous."

Mom sat down at her desk. "Well, thank

you. I take that as a compliment, coming from the famous Riot Brothers."

"Oh, before we go, I was just wondering, Mom, can I borrow a pencil?"

"Sure," she said.

Orville and I grinned at each other out of the sides of our faces. This was going to work! She was going to scream!

She opened her drawer and calmly picked up Slobber by the tail. "Sorry, Wilbur. It seems that Slobber has eaten all my pencils."

"MOM!" Orville cried. "Why can't you be an ordinary mother and scream once in a while?"

Mom tossed Slobber to me. "Who wants to be an ordinary mother?" she asked with a smile. Then she shuffled us off to the cafeteria, where we sat down with our friends.

"Be very careful with your sandwich, Orville," I said. "Remember when Mom put fake bugs in our bread?"

Orville pulled apart his sandwich. "Just

peanut butter and jelly . . . the way I like it."
He held his hand over the goop and frowned.

"What's up?" I asked.

"This is odd," he said. "The peanut butter feels very hot to me. Like it would burn if I touched it. Does it feel hot to you?"

I put my hand over his open sandwich, and he pushed my hand into the peanut-buttery goop. "April fool!" He laughed. "I told you I'd get you when you least expected it."

"Not too shabby, Orville." I wiped my fingers while he poured out the rest of his lunch.

"Ooh!" he said. "A mini peanut butter cup! I love those." He tore it open . . . and screamed. An eyeball rolled out.

"Gotcha, O-bro!" I picked up Frank, my fake eyeball, and laughed.

FIVE
Read This Title Now
(Ha ha! I control you!)

Time was running out. The school day ended, and we hadn't fooled Mom. We tried to fool her with Plans #4 through 7 when we got home after school, and those pranks didn't work either.

I know what you're thinking. You're thinking, please tell us what did you try?

Okay.

Here's the entire list, including the ones we tried before school.

TRICKS WE TRIED

1. *Sugar and salt switcheroo.*
2. *Fake injury.*
3. *Slobber in desk drawer.*
4. *Real dollar bill glued to sidewalk.*
5. *Saying, "Your shoelace is untied."*
6. *Whoopee cushion on chair at dinner table.*
7. *Fake letter in the mailbox saying, "You won $100,000,000!"*

WARNINGS ABOUT THESE TRICKS

1. *Don't forget to switch it back, or you'll be sorry.*
2. *Ketchup stains . . . and you have to clean it up.*
3. *You need a fake rat for this one, but go ahead and invest because they make great pets.*

4. *Use a fake dollar . . . and do NOT use superglue. Mom didn't fall for it, and now we can't get it off the sidewalk.*

5. *Don't bother if your mom is wearing shoes without laces.*

6. *Make sure your brother doesn't sit on it first.*

7. *Make sure your brother doesn't open it first.*

After dinner, we had to do our homework. I had to fill out a science worksheet. Orville had to study spelling and vocabulary words.

"I would like to write all my words on the ceiling of my bedroom," Orville said. "And then I could learn them just by lying in bed and staring up at them."

I pictured Mom finding Orville's masterpiece on the ceiling . . . and it gave me a great idea. "I've got it!" I whispered.

"Got what?"

"Plan Number Eight."

"What is it?"

"Get a paintbrush and some paint. Saunter past Mom so she sees what you've got, and then go to our room."

"What do I do with the paint?"

"Nothing."

"Sounds like an odd plan, Wilbur."

"You'll see. Just give her the old Riot Brother I'm-Not-Doing-Anything-Suspicious look to make her suspicious. And I'll follow up."

"Bingo bongo, Wilbur."

I peeked around the corner from the dining room to the kitchen. Orville got a paintbrush and some paint and sauntered past Mom, who was in the kitchen.

"Hiya, Mom. What are you doing?" Orville asked innocently.

"Paying the bills, as usual," she said as she ripped a check out of her checkbook.

"You should've named me Bill," he said.

"Why?"

"Because everybody always pays Bills."

Mom had to laugh.

"Well, see you later," Orville said.

"What are you doing with that paintbrush, Orville?" she asked.

"Oh, nothing." Orville left the room.

Mom wrinkled her brow and turned back to her desk.

I tiptoed upstairs.

Orville was sitting on his bed.

"Great job! Now, watch!"

I took a big breath, then I shouted, "MOM, come quick! Orville is painting his spelling words on the ceiling!"

Orville grinned.

Mom came running up. "Orville, you are in big trouble—"

We both smiled like angels. "April fool!"

She rolled her eyes.

The Riot Brothers never fail!

The End

APRIL FOOL!
It's not the end.
There's one more chapter!

SIX

Slobbery Sleep

Poor old Mom congratulated us and went back to her boring bills. Orville and I celebrated by sliding down the hallway in our socky feet, which was so much fun we couldn't stop.

"Stop!" I finally yelled.

"I can't!" Orville cried as he slid by.

"You must!" I dumped laundry from the hamper into the hallway, and when Orville came sliding back he crash-landed in the mound of stinky clothes.

"I am sorry to interrupt the fun, but we need to have a moment of appreciation for these terrific treats for our feet otherwise known as our socks." I looked down at our feet. "Thanks, guys. You never complain. You don't even mind being close up to our stinky feet! Let's hear it for our socks!"

"Hip hip hooray!" Orville shouted.

I twirled around on my slippery feet. "Can you imagine slipping your bare tootsies into anything else, Orville? How about paper bags?"

"No!" Orville yelled and started slip-sliding around.

"Rubber gloves?"

"No!"

"Beehives?"

"No!"

"Pumpkins full of peanut butter?"

Orville stopped. "Actually, that could be fun," he said.

We didn't have any pumpkins full of peanut butter, so I suggested that we play Swat-a-Lot.

"What-a-lot?" Orville asked.

"Swat-a-Lot! You forgot? We invented it after your birthday party last year."

As soon as I blew up a balloon, Orville remembered. We kneeled on our beds and put our socks on our hands. The important thing is to make your socks dangle. This gives you good swattage-ability. The object of the game is to see how long you can swat the balloon back and forth to each other without you or the balloon touching the ground.

"Ready or not, here I swat!" I threw a balloon into the air and, with my dangling right-handed sock, swatted it over to Orville.

He returned the balloon, putting a cottony spin on it. Low and inside.

"Sweet swat!" I cried, diving to the foot of my bed. I swatted it up and over his head.

"Great Scott! What a shot!" he replied, and jumped up to get it.

We counted each swat.

"We're up to eight. Keep it coming, Orville!" I shouted as I nailed a curve.

Nine . . . ten . . . eleven . . .

Orville's hit was high and outside—oh no! A left-handed swat would be required! I grabbed my bedpost and leaned out. With a mighty swing, I reached out with my left . . . and got it!

"Twelve!"

Orville returned with a fly.

Mom walked in and caught it. "That's enough, boys! Get to bed right now!"

"But it's not even bedtime and—"

"No buts about it!"

Sadly we pulled our socks off our hands.

"April fool!" Mom said. Then she tickled our bare tootsies. And that was really . . .

The End

P.S. We snuck Slobber under Mom's pillow. So we got an extra laugh when we heard her scream at her bedtime! Just remember, slobber is what goes *on top* of a pillow, and Slobber is what goes *under* a pillow.

ONE

Winkin' and Blink-in'

Orville and I were in the backyard playing Eyeballs Are Falling one Saturday morning when—

I bet you want me to stop right here and tell you how to play Eyeballs Are Falling.

Well, you'll just have to wait because Orville and I were right in the middle of our game.

I had our big old cup of eyeballs in my hands, and I was shaking those eyeballs all around. And then I yelled, "Eyeballs are falling!" and I tossed them out of the cup

onto the ground. They tumbled and rolled this way and that. Some of them landed with the eyeballs facing the dirt. Some of them landed with the eyeballs staring back at me. I got to keep all the eyeballs that were facing up. "Five!" I said as I plucked out my keepers.

Orville scooped up the remaining eyeballs and put them back in the cup. It was his turn.

Where can you get a whole cupful of real eyeballs to play with, you ask? Well, that's a slimy and disgusting question. We don't use real eyeballs! We use rocks, of course, and we draw the eyes on with markers. We invented this game when we were the only kids at a party for grown-ups. The party was in a backyard, which was big enough to play soccer in, but everybody just stood around in the middle of all that beautiful grass talking and staring at each other's eyeballs. So we found a bunch of rocks and turned them into eyeballs and made up this game.

Anyway, back to the story. It was Orville's turn. He tossed. Eight eyeballs stared up at him! He raised an eyebrow and laughed his evil laugh: *"Moi-ha-ha.* I must now collect my eyeballs!"

"That gives me an idea for a mission!" I said. We had been racking our brains all morning trying to come up with a good one.

"We're going to collect eyeballs?" Orville asked.

"No. We're going to become mad scientists!" I laughed my evil laugh. *"Mee-he-he."*

"Not too shabby, Wilbur."

"Thank you, Orville. Let's get going. We've got a lot of mad scientisting to do."

"But I'm winning. . . ."

"My point exactly."

TWO

The Good Thing About Getting a Tomato Thrown in Your Face

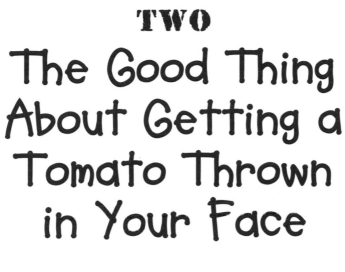

Question: What is the first thing a mad scientist needs?

Answer: Breakfast.

"Let's plan our mad scientist experiments and eat at the same time," I suggested. "But we have to keep quiet so Mom doesn't hear."

"Let's eat in our secret Riot Brother Hideout!"

"Great idea, Orville. But there's only one problem. We don't have one."

"Then let's pick a place that Mom wouldn't suspect."

We had breakfast in the bathtub. While Orville munched on an apple, I wrote our mission in the *Secret Riot Brother Mission Book*.

Orville stopped in mid-chew. "So what do mad scientists do?"

I grabbed the apple and took a bite. "They morph stuff together to create new creatures. For example, we could morph you with a cockroach and then you'd have six legs and those freaky antennae sticking out of your head."

"I don't like cockroaches. I'd rather be morphed with something I like. How about a cheetah?" He grabbed the apple back.

"Be reasonable, Orville. Where are we going to find a cheetah?" While Orville finished the apple, I made some sketches of morphs.

SCIENTIFIC SKETCHES BY WILBUR

Orville morphed with a Cat
Orville morphed with a Gnat
Orville morphed with a Rat

"Cool," Orville said. "But what if the cat or gnat or rat doesn't want to be morphed?"

"Good point, O-bro. How about we morph you with an object so you can become something useful?"

Orville morphed with a Baseball Bat
Orville morphed with a Doormat

Then I made a sketch of a Morphing Machine.

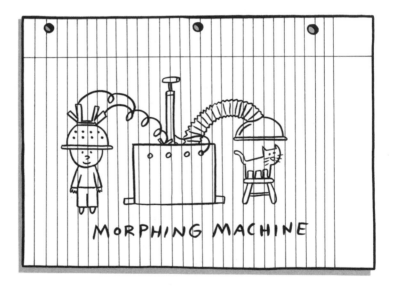

MORPHING MACHINE

"Perhaps I'll let you go first," Orville said.

"Perhaps we should let a friend go first," I suggested. "Let's find a victim—I mean, a volunteer. But first we must put on our mad scientist outfits."

I found white shirts in Mom's closet that looked like lab coats, and we put those on.

"Now for the gel!" I said.

"Gel?" Orville asked.

I pulled him into the bathroom and slathered gel on his hair to make it stick up. "Mad scientists always look as if they've just been zapped with superconducto-currents. See?"

It was a good thing our mission wasn't just to *look* like mad scientists, because the story would have been over right then and there.

We ran over to Jonathan Kemp's house. We could hear their new puppy yelping and jumping on the door. "Remember, we have to keep our mission a secret," I whispered. "So let's just ask him if he wants to come over and play."

Tiffany, Jonathan's two-year-old sister, opened the door, with the puppy jumping at her feet.

"Hi!" we said. "Can Jonathan—"

Tiffany took one look at us and screamed. "MOMMY!" The puppy ran. Tiffany ran, too.

A moment later, Mrs. Kemp peeked through the window, holding a frying pan. Then she came to the door. "Oh, it's you two. Tiffany, the bad guys are just Wilbur and Orville, see? Sorry guys, Jonathan is getting a haircut. Looks like you two could use haircuts too!"

We tried Margaret's house next. Luckily she answered.

"You guys look . . . a little crazier than usual," she said.

"Want to come over and *play*?" I asked.

"Yeah, we don't think we will give you any permanent brain damage," Orville added helpfully.

"Uh—I think I value my life too much," Margaret said. "Maybe next time."

Orville and I headed home. "Perhaps we shouldn't experiment with intelligent beings," I said.

At that very moment, we passed Goliath Hyke's house.

We stopped. I looked at Orville. Orville looked at me. "Are you thinking what I'm thinking?" I asked.

He nodded. We knocked on the door and backed up. You don't just stand in Goliath Hyke's doorway and ask him over to play if you value your life.

Nobody answered. We were about to

leave when Goliath stuck his head out a window. "What do you guys think it is . . . Halloween?" he bellowed.

"Hi, Goliath, old buddy, we're just wondering if you'd like to—"

A bright red object came flying out the window right at us. Quickly I held up my hands and caught it.

A tomato.

(Note: When you catch a tomato, try not to grip it hard in your fingers or it will explode and then your white lab coat will no longer be very white.)

"Gee thanks," I said, wiping slimy seeds off my arm.

"Does that mean you don't want to play?" Orville called out.

Goliath threw something else at Orville. It bounced off Orville's forehead and landed on the ground with a *thunk*. An apple.

"No thanks!" Orville called. "I already ate one today."

I picked up the poor bruised apple. An idea was beginning to sprout in my brain. "Orville, we've got our volunteers right here! If we blend seeds from one plant with seeds from another and pour the mixture in the ground, we could grow morphed fruits and veggies. A tomato morphed with a green pepper could make a peppery green tomato. We could call it a *peppato*. An apple morphed with a raspberry could make cute little apple-flavored raspberries. We could call them *raspapples*. A watermelon morphed with a grape could make a huge grape-flavored watermelon. We could call that a *grapelon.*"

"A brilliant idea, Wilbur. Hey, Goliath!" Orville called out. "Got any watermelons?"

I pulled Orville away.

"But I like watermelon," Orville complained.

"Do you like it on your head?"

Orville patted the top of his head. "Good point, Wilbur."

It's not every day one brother gets the chance to save another from flying fruit.

THREE
What's Growing in Your Backyard?

Our mom was in the garden pulling weeds around the daffodils when we arrived home from Goliath's Fortress of Fruit.

"Hey, we'd like to do a little planting ourselves," I said.

She looked at us as if we had mushed tomatoes in our brains rather than on our coats. "Since when do you guys like working in the garden?"

Orville pulled me aside and whispered, "Yeah, are you nuts? I don't want to work in the garden. Besides, we have a mission to accomplish."

I pulled Orville farther aside and whispered, "We're not really *gardening.* . . . We're experimenting by planting seed mixtures, remember? Grapelons? Raspapples?"

Orville nodded. "Oh yeah, I forgot!"

Before Mom could give us any weed-related chores, we ran inside and raided the refrigerator for fruits and veggies.

In pots and pans and bowls, we mushed together every seedy thing we had, and then we took those mixtures into the backyard. We dug little holes, poured the various mix-

tures in, and covered them up again with dirt.

After we filled the last hole, Orville and I sat down and stared at the ground.

"How long does it take for stuff to grow?" Orville asked.

"I don't know."

A little breeze ruffled the highest leaves on our cherry tree. Otherwise the day was very still.

Orville sighed. "Well, if it doesn't work, at least there's a bright side."

"What's the bright side?"

"We just provided a whole bunch of worms with gourmet smoothies!"

"How true, Orville. I bet if worms had lips, they'd be licking those lips right now."

Orville nodded and licked his lips. "I like worms, but if you ever morph me with a worm, Wilbur, leave me my lips, okay?"

"Sure thing, O-bro. Lips are great. They are very important if you want to make funny

faces." I sucked my cheeks in and wiggled my lips like a fish.

"Yeah." He made giant lips by folding his bottom lip over and sticking his tongue over his top lip.

We practiced sneering for a while by lifting one corner of our top lips, which is always worth doing, and then Orville stopped. "Wilbur," he said, "do you have the feeling that we are being watched?"

I looked around. All the eyeballs from our game this morning were in a pile in the dirt nearby, staring at us like we were the crazy ones.

I sneered at Orville. Orville sneered at me. "Are you prepared to lose?" I asked.

He rolled his eyes. "Ha! Let the game begin!"

FOUR
Let Those Dishes Get Stinky

Mom dragged us into the kitchen and pointed at the pile of dirty pots and bowls. "Okay, what is this?"

Orville looked at our poor old mother and then he looked at me. "Mom is getting so old she doesn't even remember what dirty dishes are," he sighed. "That's so sad." Then he added in a whisper, "Maybe we should experiment with her brain."

Mom rolled her eyes. "I know what dirty

dishes are, Orville. I meant, why is the kitchen so messy?"

He grinned. "Well, why didn't you say so? It's messy because we're mad—"

He was about to give away our mission, so I elbowed him. "We're just mad . . . because someone left dirty dishes in the sink, aren't we Orville?" I gave him the secret Riot Brother wink.

Orville got it and looked suitably horrified. "Yes, we are mad! I can't imagine who has done such a dirtifying thing."

Mom put her hands on her hips. "*I* can imagine! And I can imagine just who is going to clean it up right now."

"Who?" Orville asked.

"You and your brother!"

I looked at the pile of dirty pots. "Mom, if children were meant to wash dishes, sinks would be lower," I argued.

"Honey, that's why footstools were invented." She pushed a stool over to me with her foot and left the kitchen without even waiting to hear the rest of my argument. I didn't have one, but it would have been nice of her to wait.

"I'm thinking we should morph her with a footstool and sell her to someone with very stinky feet," Orville muttered.

"I heard that," Mom called.

I whispered, "We should morph her with something that doesn't have ears." Orville squeezed in next to me on the stool and squirted dishwashing soap into the sink. We watched the sink fill up with soap-bubbly water, and then we swished our hands around in the warm foam.

"It's a crying shame that this beautiful water has to be polluted with dirty dishes," he said.

I nodded. "Maybe while we wait for the fruitmorphs to grow, we should do a mad scientist experiment to invent something you can cook and eat without any dishes."

"Food you cook in your mouth," Orville said.

"I've got it! How about we experiment with macaroni and cheese to make it boil in your mouth? No pots! No plates! No microwave! You don't even need a fork!"

Orville started yelling hooray and blowing foam in the air until Mom called out from the living room, "Sounds like you're having way too much fun in there!"

"Shhh. Remember Riot Brother Rule Number Twenty-three. If you're having fun when you're supposed to be doing a chore, do it quietly so the grown-ups won't get suspicious."

"Hooray!" Orville whispered, and put a glob of foam on the end of his nose.

"Come on, these dirty dishes aren't going anywhere. Let's design an eye-catching box before we experiment with the macaroni."

Maybe you can't judge a book by the cover,

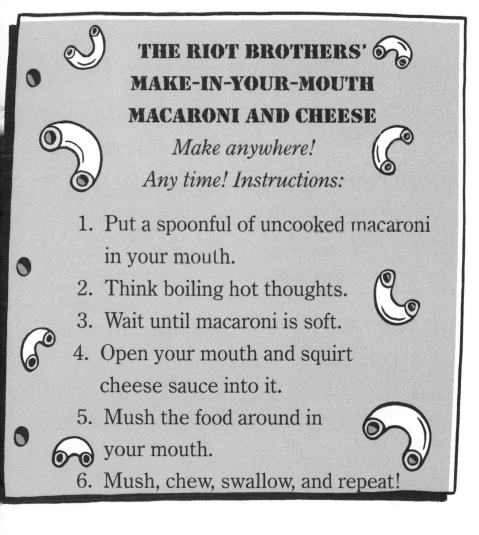

THE RIOT BROTHERS'
MAKE-IN-YOUR-MOUTH
MACARONI AND CHEESE
Make anywhere!
Any time! Instructions:

1. Put a spoonful of uncooked macaroni in your mouth.
2. Think boiling hot thoughts.
3. Wait until macaroni is soft.
4. Open your mouth and squirt cheese sauce into it.
5. Mush the food around in your mouth.
6. Mush, chew, swallow, and repeat!

but you sure can judge mac-n-cheese by the box. And ours looked *goooooooooooooood.*

"Let's make a TV commercial to go with it!" I suggested. We set up the movie camera. "Hold up our box and pretend you're eating the most delicious thing in the world," I told Orville. "Action!"

While Orville chewed, I filmed a close-up of his mouth and made up these lines on the spot, which I said in a very fun, TV-guy voice. "Why do grown-ups say you can't talk with your mouth full? Orville and I do it all the time. Sometimes the food falls out and

lands on the floor, but isn't that why brooms were invented? I mean, think about the poor brooms of the world. What if they had nothing to clean up? They'd be miserable. So, do the brooms of the world a favor; sit down at the family table and talk with your mouth open." Orville grabbed a broom and started dancing with it. "But NOT when you're eating The Riot Brothers' Make-in-Your-Mouth Macaroni and Cheese!" He threw the broom aside. "When you're eating our newest creation, you won't want to miss a bite!" He kept his mouth closed, grinned, and rubbed his tummy.

"CUT!" I said. "It's a take!"

"Wow! That was fun," Orville said. "But now I'm hungry. Let's try our experiment."

Just then Mom walked in. Unfortunately for us, in addition to having big ears, our mom also has lousy timing and a really sensitive nose. "I smell dirty dishes," she said.

"We'll do them soon."

"You'll do them now."

"But we're being creative, Mom," Orville said. "You always like it when we're creative."

"I feel a saying coming on," I said.

"Oh great," Mom said. I think she really loves my sayings.

I cleared my throat. "Dishes stinking in your sink prove your child knows how to think."

"How true," Orville said. "And it rhymes, too!"

"Your sayings should be made into bumper stickers, Wilbur," Mom said.

"What a great idea!" I exclaimed.

"I was just kidding, Wilbur. Get a sponge and get busy."

"Mom, not only are we going to wash the dishes, but after our secret experiment is over, we will be able to serve you a delicious dinner that will require no cleaning up what-soever."

"I guess it's my lucky day," she said. Sometimes, she actually says something that makes sense.

FIVE

Meet Mr. Huffy and Mr. Spitter

Finally, the stinking dishes were clean, and we could begin our experiment. I had a stopwatch. We had to see how long it would take to boil macaroni in our mouths so that we could put the right number of minutes on the box.

"On your mark, get set, boil!" I clicked on the stopwatch.

Orville put a spoonful of raw macaroni in his mouth.

"We have to get the inside of you boiling. Think about an erupting volcano," I suggested. "Imagine the red-hot lava!" I looked at Orville's face. He looked too peaceful. Time was wasting. What would make Orville boil on the inside? *Think, think, think.*

If it ever seems to you that I'm having trouble finding an answer to a question, it is only because my brain is like the size of Alaska, which happens to be the largest state of all. Hey, here's a great idea: If you ever get this question on a test—What is the largest state?—just remember that my brain is the same size as Alaska, and you will get a good grade.

Well, I searched my humongous brain, and I came up with a great idea. I could insult Orville, which would make him boiling mad. I thought for a moment. "Orville, you're so clueless, you'd try to chop down a beanstalk with a toothbrush."

He started to laugh. I had to think up something more insulting.

"Orville, you're so ugly, you make the Big Bad Wolf look good. You're not Prince Charming, you're Prince Alarming."

He stuck out his hands like claws and raised his eyebrows wolfishly.

I sighed. "Orville, you're not supposed to like being called clueless and ugly."

Orville spit out the macaroni. "But it's a fun game. I want to play."

"It's not a game. I was insulting you!"

"Well, we could make it a game. The Insult Me Game."

"We're not playing games, Orville! We're doing a mad scientist experiment."

"Well, you don't have to get all huffy about it, Mr. Huffy."

"Well, you're not supposed to spit out the macaroni, Mr. Spitter!"

"Well, you try, Dr. Perfect Scientist."

"Well, I can do better than you, Dr. Perfect Spitter."

Mom walked in. "Looks like I've got a couple of mad scientists in my kitchen."

I almost fell off my chair. "Orville, are you mad?"

"Yeah."

"Me too! Isn't that great? We accomplished our mission."

"But we didn't get the macaroni to boil in our mouths."

"That wasn't our mission. Our mission was to become mad scientists. We're scientists because we're experimenting, and we're mad because we insulted each other. So we're mad scientists."

Orville jumped up. "We did it!" We danced around the kitchen in a very madly scientific way.

Mom looked at the pile of slobbered-over macaroni on the table. "I just have one question," she added. "Is this what you guys are planning for dinner?"

"Yes!" Orville said. "We're mad, mad, mad!"

"I think I'll order a pizza," she said.

Are you making a note of this? If you ever want your mom to order a pizza but are afraid she'll say no, just make something slobbery for her. She'll be dialing the pizza place faster than you can say "Have a mug of mushed-up macaroni and mucus, Mom."

SIX
Rumpus Bumpus

The pizza was delicious. After dinner Mom made us de-goop our hair and wash the lab coats.

"Hey, look!" Orville called me over to the window. Jonathan, Margaret, Tiffany, and the puppy were frolicking out in the Kemps' front yard. The puppy was chasing fireflies, and everybody was laughing.

"Man, I'd like to morph with a firefly!" Orville said.

"Because you want to be puppy chow?"

"No. Because I want a flashing rump."

That gave me an idea. "Orville, let's invent pajamas with a flashing light in the rear end."

"Bingo bongo, Wilbur! Let the flashing rumpus begin!"

We got flashlights, stuffed them down our underpants, and ran outside.

"Check it out, guys!" Orville cried, and wiggled his glowing rear. "We're fireflies."

"Firefries!" Tiffany yelled, and started jumping up and down, which is what she does when she's really excited.

We ran over to Jonathan's yard, and the puppy *and* Tiffany *and* Margaret *and* Jonathan chased us around and around. The darker it grew outside, the better our bottoms looked.

Then Mr. Kemp came out. "Bedtime for all children and puppies," he said.

"And firefries," Tiffany added sadly.

"We'll be firefries again soon," Orville said, and patted her on the head.

We turned off our flashlights, walked back to our yard, and sat on our grassy hill.

Mom came out and sat next to us. "You know, it's really time for bed," she said quietly.

I sighed. "Yeah, we know." Something about knowing you have to go to bed just makes the great outdoors even greater. Warm golden lights were shining in the windows of our neighbors' houses, and I could imagine them all bumbling around inside, brushing their teeth and watching TV and washing the dishes. But we weren't bumbling around; we were sitting outside in the cool dark air, just feeling the breeze and smelling the grass and watching over the neighborhood like three secret owls.

My mind flew to the backyard, and I thought about the seed mixtures we planted earlier that day. What if they were starting to sprout in their warm little earthy hiding places? What if something brand new was being born for the very first time at this very moment?

"Mom," I asked, "how long does it take for a plant to grow from a seed?"

"Depends on the seed. Some take days. Some take weeks."

"I bet mushed-up seeds grow a lot faster,"

Orville said hopefully. Then he whispered to me, "Let's check tomorrow."

I nodded.

A firefly blinked in the distance.

"Mom," Orville said, "what if we sell our flashing rumpus pajamas and children all over the world buy them and we make a fortune?"

"Then there will be a bunch of little lightning butts running around," she said.

We all laughed. "It would be a beautiful sight," I added.

We were quiet for a moment.

"The Kemps' puppy is really cute," Orville said suddenly. "Mom, you should get us a puppy."

Mom laughed and rolled her eyes. "I think you guys are plenty."

"Is that an insult?" I asked.

She put her arms around us. "Take it as a compliment," she said.

And so we did.

And then we stuffed the flashlights down our underpants and ran around before Mom chased us up to bed.

The End

BONUS!

RIOT BROTHER GAMES

Knot-a-Sock

Here's how to play Knot-a-Sock. First you put socks on your feet. You might think that's obvious. But there are other Riot Brother Games that require putting socks on your hands, so I felt it was important to write down the feet part. Use the longest socks you have, but not soccer socks because those are too tight. Pull one of your opponent's socks off just enough to tie it in a knot at the toe. Meanwhile, he or she will be trying to grab your sock. You may thrash, but you have to control your thrashing because if you thrash too much one of you will get hurt and then your parents will be mad and you won't be able to play.

In order to win, you must get both of your

opponent's socks tied in knots before both of your socks get tied. Most often the game is planned, but you can also do a surprise attack. When the other player is wearing socks and you aren't is an excellent time for a surprise attack because then you can't lose! The loser has to do a crazy sock dance (not kidding—ha ha).

Sock Me a Story

Here's how you play: First, roll a pair of socks into a ball. Hold the ball and start telling a story starring a sock. At some point in the story, throw the sock ball to another player, who then has to add on to your story.

If you have trouble thinking up great stories, use this secret formula: Have your sock want something, then make sure something gets in the way of your sock getting what he or she wants, and then have your sock win in the end. Hooray!

Think about it. Socks never get starring

roles. It's always about the shoes. So, give your socks a thrill and make up a story about them. They'll love you for it.

Swat-a-Lot

You need a balloon, socks, and any number of players. Each player must be on some kind of base . . . like a bed or a chair. You cannot leave your base once the game begins. Make fists and put socks on your hands so that the toe part of the sock is dangling. Using the dangling part of your socks, swat the balloon to each other. If the balloon touches the floor or if you fall off your base, then the game stops. Count the number of swats. Try to get as many as you can. To make the game even more exciting, use more than one balloon. While playing, you are allowed to swiftly swerve, swish, swipe, swoop, or sway. During breaks, you are allowed to switch or swap places. If you are playing hard you may sweat, but please do not swear. This is a fun game to play in Sweden or Switzerland. But if you're not swarming to Sweden or Switzerland soon, try playing it in a swimming pool! (But don't swig any swallows of water.) However you swat, have fun because it's a swell game.

Eyeballs Are Falling

Collect as many eyeball-sized rocks as you can find. Draw an eyeball on one side of each rock with a marker. Put them all in one cup. The first person tosses out all the rocks and says, "Eyeballs are falling." The tosser gets to take whichever rocks land with the eyeballs facing up. All the rest go back in the cup, and the next player goes. Play until there are no more eyeballs left. Count up your eyeballs. Whoever has the most wins.

Note that whoever goes first has an advantage, so you must play as many rounds as you have players. For example, if you have two players, you must play at least two rounds, giving each player a chance to go first. If you have one thousand players, you must play one thousand rounds, which means you're going to need a supersized cup of eyeballs!

Insult Me Game

As you recall, Orville got the idea for this game from me! We have played it many times since then. It is perhaps the most sophisticated and difficult of all the Riot Brother Games, but I am good at it. I mean, if Making Up Insults was a subject on report cards, I'd get an A+.

To play, your opponent picks a category, and you have to think up an insult in that category. For example, you could choose Fairy Tale Insults, Insect Insults, Sports Insults, Animal Insults, or anything else.

If you are an adult reading this and you are getting all huffy, thinking how horribly awful we are for making a game out of insulting each other, please consider the educational benefits. While creating our insults, we are seriously practicing our verbal reasoning and language arts skills. Besides, we don't really mean it or get mad. We're just trying to boil our brains!

ADDITIONAL RIOT BROTHER RULES

16. You have to write down your mission of the day.
17. If you rescue a damsel in distress, you do not have to marry her.
18. If someone puts your brother down, stick up for him.
19. Always keep a flashlight under your pillow.
20. Never ever go to bed without eating dessert.
21. If your brother is ever in an embarrassing situation, help him out of it.

22. If your brother ever makes an embarrassing situation even more embarrassing while trying to help you out of it, you MUST help him in return.

23. If you're having fun when you're supposed to be doing a chore, do it quietly so the grown-ups won't get suspicious.

RIOT BROTHER SAYINGS

—Singing a song is like taking your voice on a field trip. It deserves to have a little fun.

—If someone tries to bug you, don't let it bug you.

—The great advantage to being weird most of the time is that when you are weird, no one thinks it's weird.

—The world would be a better place if all children had a roof over their head, food in their stomach, a smile in their heart, and a fake rat in their pocket.

—Dishes stinking in your sink prove your child knows how to think.

THE RIOT BROTHER GUIDE TO KNIGHTLY TALK

Old Knightly Talk	What It Means in Normal English
Alas! Alack!	Oh dear! Phooey! As in: Alas! Alack! A fly has landed in my chocolate milk.
-eth	Addeth this to the ends of your verbs to maketh your sentences soundeth medieval.
Farewell	Goodbye
Fie	Rats! As in: Fie, you have sneezed in my soup!

Goodly	Good, only better
Hark!	Listen! As in: Hark, what's that noise?
Hear ye!	Yo, listen up!
Lowly Servant	Your brother or sister (ha!)
Make haste	Hurry up
Methinks	I think. As in: Methinks I smell a skunk!
O	O Reader, just throw this in front of some one's name to make it sound fancier.
Thee/thy	You/your. As in: Get thee to thy bed.
Thou art	You are. As in: Thou art annoying.
'Tis	It is
Yonder	Over there. As in: Is that a green bean in yonder nostril?

BONUS SONGS

Flare, Flare, Flare Your Nostrils ("Row Your Boat" tune)

by Wilbur and Orville Riot

Flare,   flare,   flare your nos-trils   gent - ly   in   the

air.   Flap your arms and wig-gle your rear   on - ly

if   you   dare.

Our Pants Go Marching ("The Ants Go Marching" tune)

by Wilbur and Orville Riot

Our pants go march-ing one by one. Hur - rah! Hur - rah! Our

pants go march-ing one by one. Hur-rah! Hur-rah! Our pants go march-ing

this we swear. That's why we're in our un-der-wear. And our

pants don't care cuz now is their chance to dance. Boom Boom Boom

Boom Boom Boom Boom Boom!

Air Conditioning ("The Old Gray Mare" tune)

by Wilbur and Orville Riot

Our fine bot-toms got air con-di-tion-ing, air con-di-tion-ing,

air con-di-tion-ing. Our fine bot-toms got air con-di-tion-ing.

That's why we like to put holes in our pants!

SNEAK PEEK!

Meet Amelia E. Hart, the Riot Brothers' cousin, in:

Riot Brothers #4
Take the Mummy and Run
The Riot Brothers Are on a Roll

Orville and I opened the door and . . . guess what happened?

You'll never guess, so I'll just tell you.

We opened the door and a long green snake fell on our heads!

"Aiiiiiiiiiiii!" we screamed.

A skinny girl wearing an old aviator hat with short funny hair and a huge grin jumped out from behind our bush. "Gotcha!"

It's hard to stun the Riot Brothers, but stunned we were.

Mom stepped forward. "You must be—"

"Amelia!" the girl said. She picked up her rubber snake. "And this is my pet snake, Curly."

I looked at Orville. Orville looked at me.

"A girl with a fake snake," Orville whispered. "I think she's our kind of cousin."

Talk, talk, talk. It's all grown-ups want to do.

How was the trip? Are you hungry? How have you been?

They don't even know how to ask good questions.

Do you have any candy? Can you do anything funny with your nostrils? Was there a mini-fridge in that taxi? These are good questions.

Mom was asking question after question, and frankly, time was wasting.

"Pardon me for interrupting," I said in my excellent host voice. "We need to show Amelia where to freshen up."

I gave Amelia my secret Riot Brother wink.

Right away she got it. "Yes," she said. "I obviously need freshening."

"Looks like we've got three peas in a pod here," Mom said with a big smile.

Before Mom could talk more about vegetables, we grabbed Slobber and Curly and led Amelia into the backyard.

"I like your style," Amelia said. "What are we going to do?"

"We need to have a secret Riot Brother meeting," I said. "We are the Riot Brothers. And according to Riot Brother Rule Number Twenty-Four: Kids who are fun can become Riot Brothers even if they aren't our brothers."

"Did you just make that up?" Orville whispered.

"Yes," I whispered back.

He gave me a thumbs-up.

"Would you like to join?" I asked.

"What do you do?"

"Lots of stuff," Orville said. "We find hidden treasures and become spies and mad scientists."

"Our mission," I explained, "is to make something exciting happen every day."

"I'm in!"